DATE DUE

for Cog

Third Printing

Copyright © 1976 by Dick Gackenbach
All rights reserved. Printed in the United States of America.

Library of Congress Cataloging in Publication Data

Gackenbach, Dick.
  Claude and Pepper.

  SUMMARY: Pepper, a feisty dachshund, involves Claude
in his attempt to run away from home.
  [1. Dogs—Fiction]. I. Title.
PZ7.G117Cj   [E]   75-25507
ISBN 0-395-28793-6

CLAUDE
AND
PEPPER

WORDS AND PICTURES BY DICK GACKENBACH

 Houghton Mifflin/Clarion Books/New York

"Where are you going, Pepper?"

"I'm going off to see the great wide world, Claude!"

"Your mother will miss you, Pepper."

"I'll come home to visit someday, Claude."

"Let me walk
   down the road with you.
   O.K., Pepper?"

"O.K., Claude."

On the road they met Lila the Goose.

"Hello, Lila. How are your lovely goslings?"

"They are growing fast, Claude.
They need all my love and care."

"Isn't it
nice to
have someone
who loves
you, Pepper?"

"I guess so, Claude."

Soon they met Nora the Goat eating roses.

"Hello, Nora. That's a fine kid you have."

"Thank you, Claude. He makes me very happy,
  he loves me so."

"Isn't it
nice to
love someone,
Pepper?"

"Well, maybe, Claude."

Soon they met Helen the Chicken.

"Hello, Helen. Where are your chicks?"

"Beneath my feathers where they
are safe and warm, Claude!"

"Isn't it nice
to have
someone to
watch over
you, Pepper?"

"Yes, Claude."

They came to a school bus stop.

"Where are you going, Pepper?"

"You'll see, Claude!"